THE · WORLD · ARC

HUMAN
BODY

Michael Gabb

Consultant
Brian Ward

Illustrated by
Chris Forsey, Wendy Lewis, Pat Ludlow, Brian Pearce
Bernard Robinson, Mike Saunders, Charlotte Snook

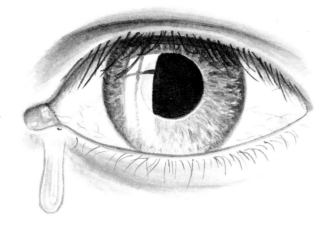

Kingfisher Books

NEW YORK

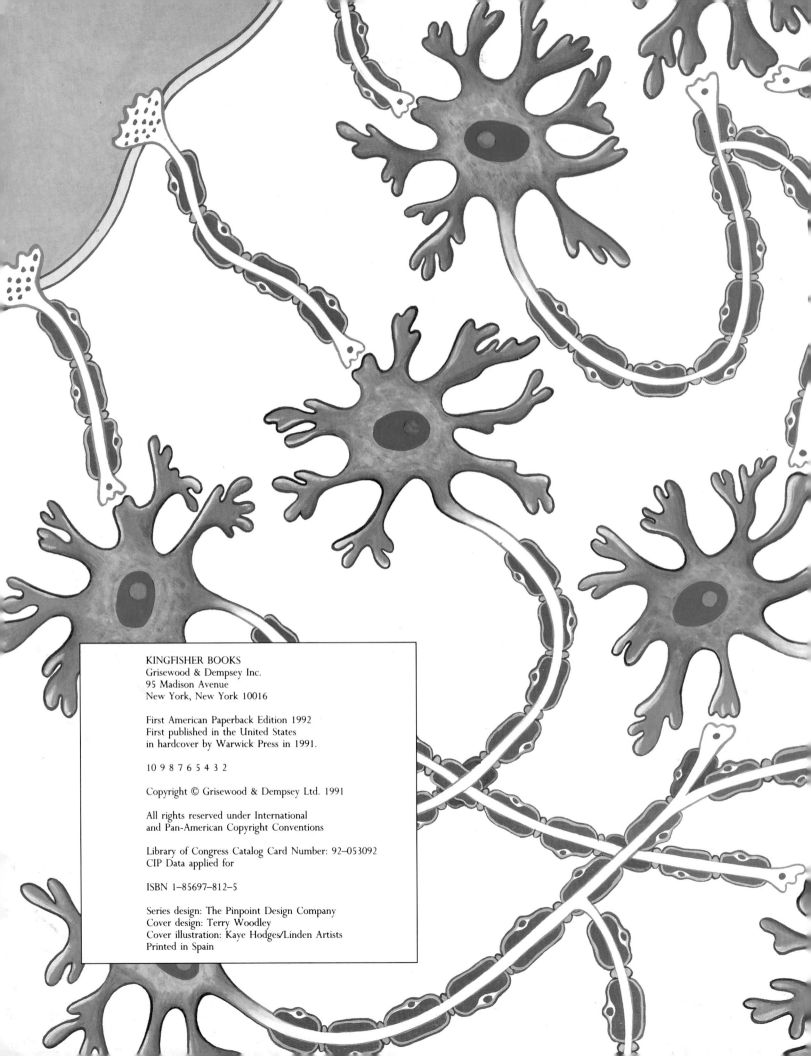

KINGFISHER BOOKS
Grisewood & Dempsey Inc.
95 Madison Avenue
New York, New York 10016

First American Paperback Edition 1992
First published in the United States
in hardcover by Warwick Press in 1991.

10 9 8 7 6 5 4 3 2

Copyright © Grisewood & Dempsey Ltd. 1991

Library of Congress Catalog Card Number: 92–053092
CIP Data applied for

ISBN 1–85697–812–5

Series design: The Pinpoint Design Company
Cover design: Terry Woodley
Cover illustration: Kaye Hodges/Linden Artists
Printed in Spain

Contents

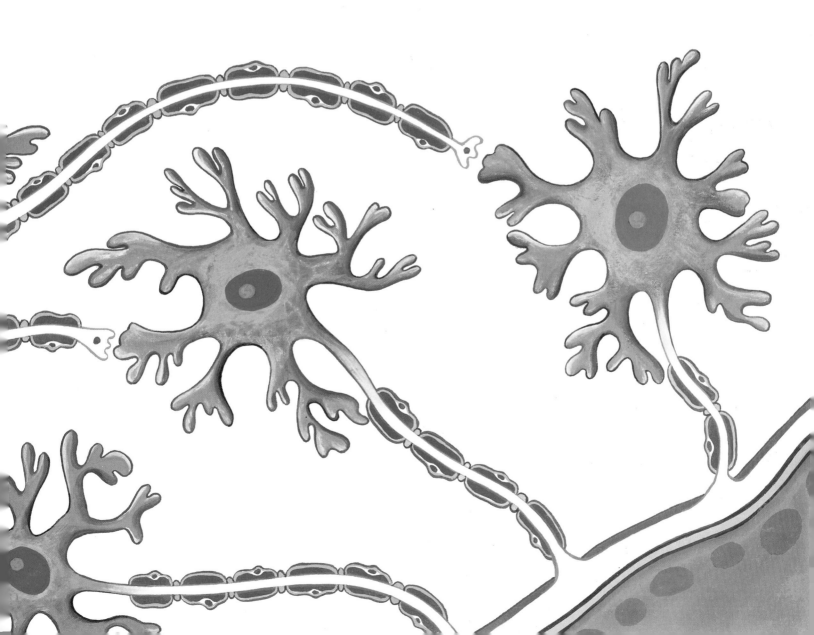

The Building Blocks of Life

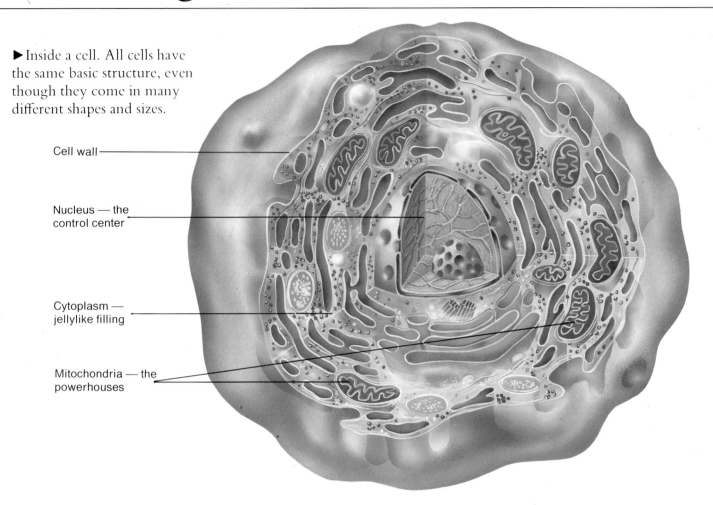

▶ Inside a cell. All cells have the same basic structure, even though they come in many different shapes and sizes.

Cell wall

Nucleus — the control center

Cytoplasm — jellylike filling

Mitochondria — the powerhouses

Our bodies are made up of millions of tiny living units called cells, most of them too small to be seen without a microscope. These cells are the building blocks from which everything else is made — blood, bones, skin, nerves, muscles, and all the other body parts.

Different Kinds of Cell

There are many types of cells in our bodies, each with its own special job to do. Brain cells are among the smallest — they measure only a ten-thousandth of an inch across. The cell with the largest body is the ovum, or egg cell. Egg cells are just large enough to be seen without a microscope.

Cells also come in different shapes — muscle cells, for example, are tube-shaped. There are also round, flat, and square cells.

What are Cells Made of?

Even though cells come in all shapes and sizes, each one is made to the same basic plan. Most cells have a control center called a nucleus, which keeps the cell alive and does its own special job.

The cell body is filled with a jellylike material called cytoplasm, in which structures called mitochondria float. These are the cell's powerhouses, where the energy needed to keep the cell alive and working is produced.

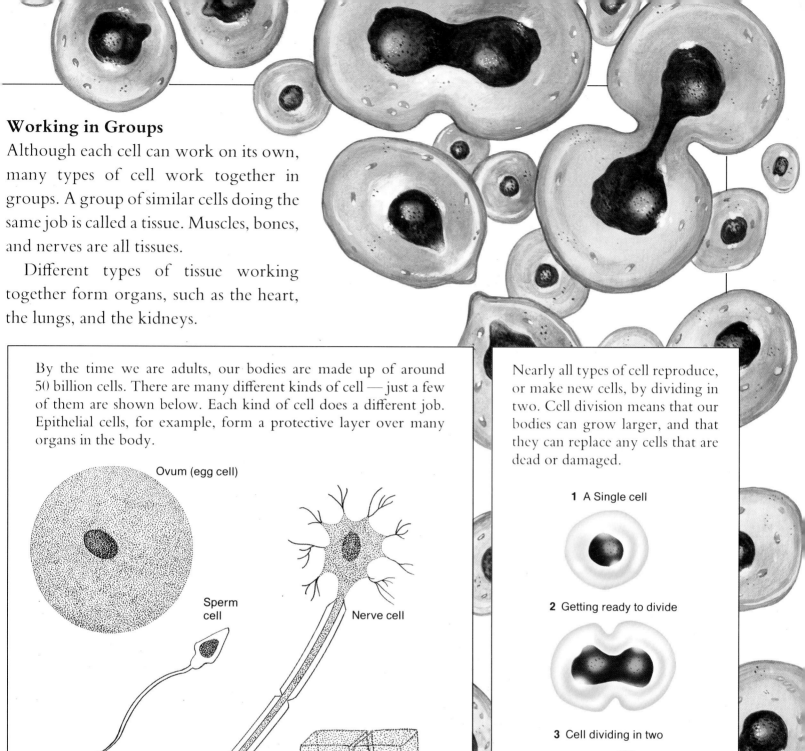

Working in Groups

Although each cell can work on its own, many types of cell work together in groups. A group of similar cells doing the same job is called a tissue. Muscles, bones, and nerves are all tissues.

Different types of tissue working together form organs, such as the heart, the lungs, and the kidneys.

By the time we are adults, our bodies are made up of around 50 billion cells. There are many different kinds of cell — just a few of them are shown below. Each kind of cell does a different job. Epithelial cells, for example, form a protective layer over many organs in the body.

Ovum (egg cell)

Sperm cell

Nerve cell

Epithelial cells

Muscle cell

Nearly all types of cell reproduce, or make new cells, by dividing in two. Cell division means that our bodies can grow larger, and that they can replace any cells that are dead or damaged.

1 A Single cell

2 Getting ready to divide

3 Cell dividing in two

4 After division – two new cells

Every Move You Make

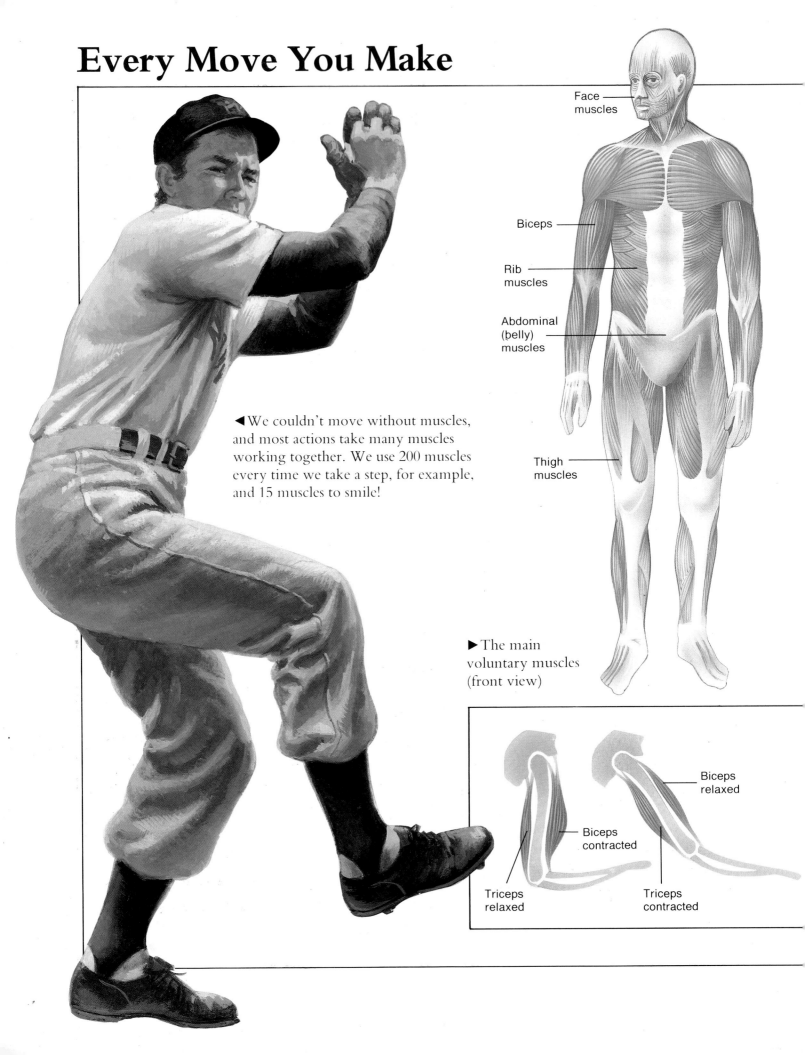

◄We couldn't move without muscles, and most actions take many muscles working together. We use 200 muscles every time we take a step, for example, and 15 muscles to smile!

Face muscles

Biceps

Rib muscles

Abdominal (belly) muscles

Thigh muscles

►The main voluntary muscles (front view)

Biceps relaxed

Biceps contracted

Triceps relaxed

Triceps contracted

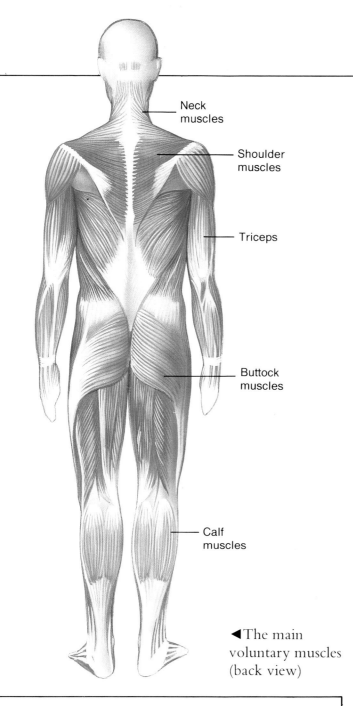

Neck muscles

Shoulder muscles

Triceps

Buttock muscles

Calf muscles

◀The main voluntary muscles (back view)

Muscles can't push, they can only pull, so they often work in pairs. One muscle shortens to pull a bone one way. Then another muscle pulls the bone back again.

To bend the arm, the biceps muscle contracts and pulls up the radius bone. To straighten it, the biceps relaxes and the triceps contracts.

Muscles are pulling gently against one another most of the time. This keeps them firm and stops them from becoming floppy. Muscles get bigger and stronger if you exercise them.

All the movements you make depend on muscles. Even when you are standing still, muscles in your back, neck, arms, and legs are working to keep you upright.

You have over 650 muscles. Some are large and powerful, and easy to see. But others are tiny and hidden from view, like the ones you use to blink or to change the expression on your face.

How Do Muscles Work?

Muscles can only move in two ways. They can contract, or tighten, and they can relax, or loosen. This means that they can pull, but they can't push. Most muscles work in pairs because of this — one pulling one way, the other pulling the opposite way.

Muscles are joined to bones by tough "bands" called tendons. As muscles contract, tendons pull the bones and make them move.

Two Sorts of Muscle

Most muscles can be controlled by thinking about them — they move when you want them to. They are called voluntary muscles and there are more than 600 of them.

Other muscles work automatically, without you thinking about them. They are called involuntary muscles, and they include the heart and the muscles you use to breathe and to digest food.

The heart is completely different from any other muscle in your body, because it works without stopping or tiring throughout your whole life.

Framing Up

You have more than 200 bones in your body, and the framework they make is called the skeleton. Without this framework of bones to support it and carry its weight, your body would collapse.

Where Bones Meet

The place where two bones meet is called a joint. Some are fixed, but others can move. The skull has fixed joints — most of the 29 bones in it are fused together, and only the jaw bone can move.

Other joints allow more movement. The backbone is made up of 26 small bones called vertebrae. These have sliding joints which allow you to bend your back and to turn your head. Other types of moving joint are called hinge joints and ball-and-socket joints.

Many joints are "oiled" by a liquid called synovial fluid. This allows the bones to move smoothly against each other and keeps wear and tear to a minimum.

Inside a Bone

Bones aren't solid. They are like strong tubes with blood and other living material inside them. Each bone has two layers. The hard outer layer is called compact bone. The inner layer looks like a honeycomb, but it is still very strong. It's called spongy bone.

What are Bones Made of?

Bones are hard and strong because they are partly made of stony substances called minerals. Before we were born, though, all of our bones began as a rubbery material called cartilage.

As children grow, cartilage is constantly being formed at the end of their bones. When the cartilage hardens it makes new bone. Some of the cartilage remains, however, to cushion the heads of the bones.

Even when we are adults, some body parts — including our noses and outer ears — are made completely of cartilage and not bone.

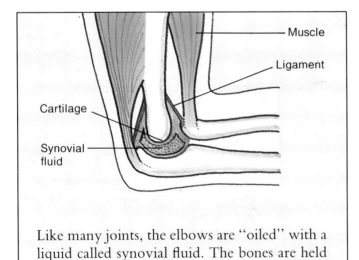

Like many joints, the elbows are "oiled" with a liquid called synovial fluid. The bones are held together by straps called ligaments, and their heads are cushioned with rubbery cartilage.

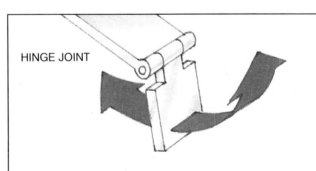

Hinge joints are moving joints that bend and straighten — just like a door swinging on its hinges. Like door hinges, though, these joints can only bend in one direction.

You have hinge joints at your knees and elbows, and between the bones in your fingers.

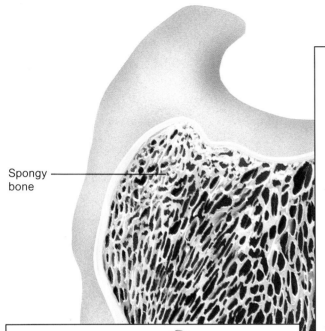

Spongy bone

BALL-AND-SOCKET JOINT

In ball–and–socket joints, the round end of one bone fits into a hollow in another bone. This allows all-around movement.

You have ball-and-socket joints at your shoulders and hips, so your limbs can move freely in most directions.

Although most adults have 206 bones, all of us are born with about 350. Many of the smaller bones join together as we grow older.

The longest bone in the body is the femur, or thigh bone. The smallest is only about a tenth of an inch long. It's called the stirrup bone and it is in the ear.

Some bones protect important parts of the body. For example, the cranium forms a bony case around the brain. The heart and lungs are protected by 12 pairs of rib bones, while the 26 vertebrae in the spine protect nerves that run from the brain down the back.

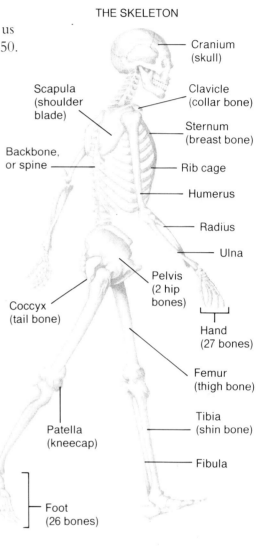

THE SKELETON

- Cranium (skull)
- Scapula (shoulder blade)
- Clavicle (collar bone)
- Sternum (breast bone)
- Backbone, or spine
- Rib cage
- Humerus
- Radius
- Ulna
- Pelvis (2 hip bones)
- Coccyx (tail bone)
- Hand (27 bones)
- Femur (thigh bone)
- Tibia (shin bone)
- Patella (kneecap)
- Fibula
- Foot (26 bones)

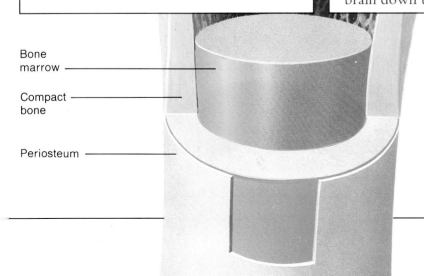

Bone marrow

Compact bone

Periosteum

◄Bones are covered in a thin skin called the periosteum. Then comes an outer layer of hard compact bone and, inside that, a layer of spongy bone.

The long bones of the arms and legs have a hollow center filled with bone marrow. The bone marrow is where most blood cells are made — around 200 billion red blood cells are produced every day!

The Body Pump

Your heart is a powerful muscle which pumps blood around your body. It is only the size of your fist and it weighs less than a pound (0.5 kg). Every day it pumps about 2,000 gallons of blood around you, yet you aren't normally aware that it is beating! Run quickly upstairs, though, and you'll soon feel it thumping away inside your rib cage.

What is Blood?

Although blood looks red, it is largely made up of a yellowish liquid called plasma. This liquid carries dissolved food particles called nutrients to all the cells in the body.

Different sorts of blood cells float in the plasma — red cells, white cells, and tiny bits of cell called platelets. The red blood cells contain a substance called hemoglobin which is the body's oxygen carrier. It is hemoglobin which colors the red cells in blood.

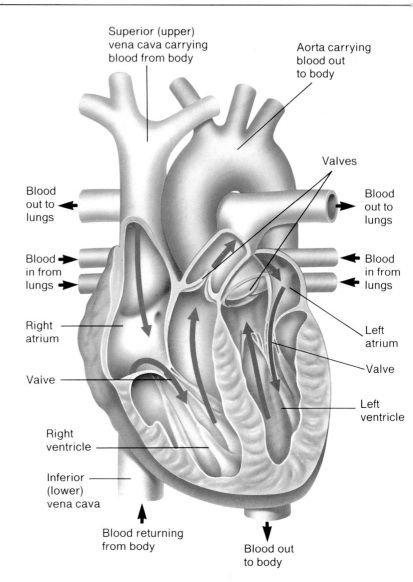

Superior (upper) vena cava carrying blood from body

Aorta carrying blood out to body

Valves

Blood out to lungs

Blood out to lungs

Blood in from lungs

Blood in from lungs

Right atrium

Left atrium

Vaive

Valve

Right ventricle

Left ventricle

Inferior (lower) vena cava

Blood returning from body

Blood out to body

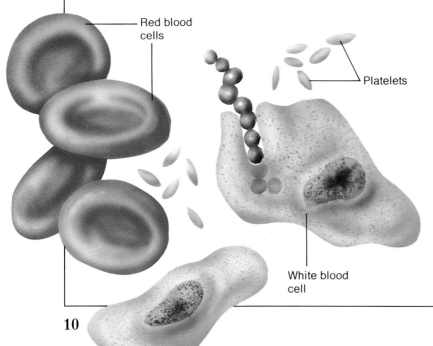

Red blood cells

Platelets

White blood cell

▲ The heart has four main chambers — left and right atrium, and left and right ventricle.

Blood from the head and body flows into the right atrium and down into the right ventricle. From there it is pumped to the lungs to pick up oxygen. It then flows into the left atrium and down into the left ventricle. When this contracts, the blood is forced out of the heart and through the main arteries at a speed of more than 60 feet (18 m) a minute!

◀There are several types of white cell. Their main job is to fight the diseases that make us ill.

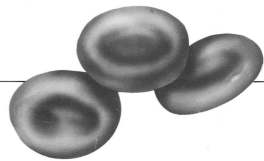

10

The Blood System

Blood flows around the body in a network of vessels, or tubes. There are three main types of blood vessel. The ones called arteries carry blood containing nutrients and oxygen. They take blood from the heart to all the cells in the body.

Arteries divide and become smaller and smaller, until eventually they split into millions of tiny vessels called capillaries. These deliver nutrients and oxygen to the body cells and collect waste materials.

The capillaries then gradually join up into larger blood vessels called veins, which return the blood to the heart. From there the blood is pumped to the lungs to pick up more oxygen, and the whole cycle starts again.

The blood in the veins travels quite slowly, and many large veins have valves to stop blood from draining back-ward toward the legs and feet.

Blood flowing forward forces the valve flaps open (1). Blood flowing back forces them shut (2). The valves in the heart work in the same way.

Blood is also helped along by the arm and leg muscles contracting. That's why, if you stand still for a long time, blood can collect in your legs and make them puffy and sore.

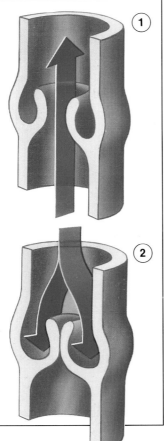

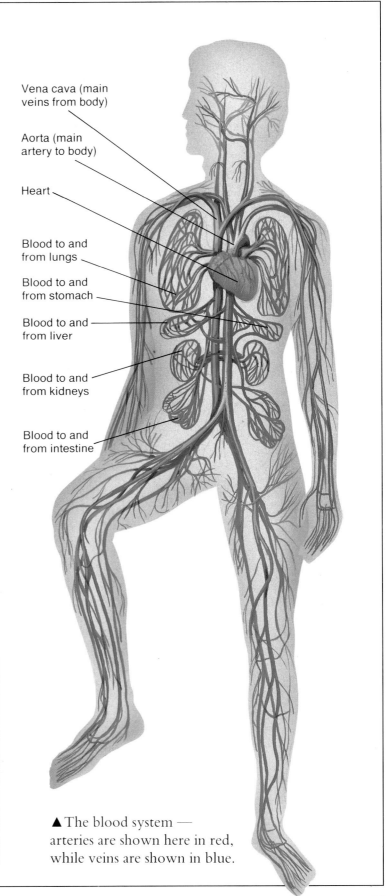

Vena cava (main veins from body)

Aorta (main artery to body)

Heart

Blood to and from lungs

Blood to and from stomach

Blood to and from liver

Blood to and from kidneys

Blood to and from intestine

▲ The blood system — arteries are shown here in red, while veins are shown in blue.

The Body at War

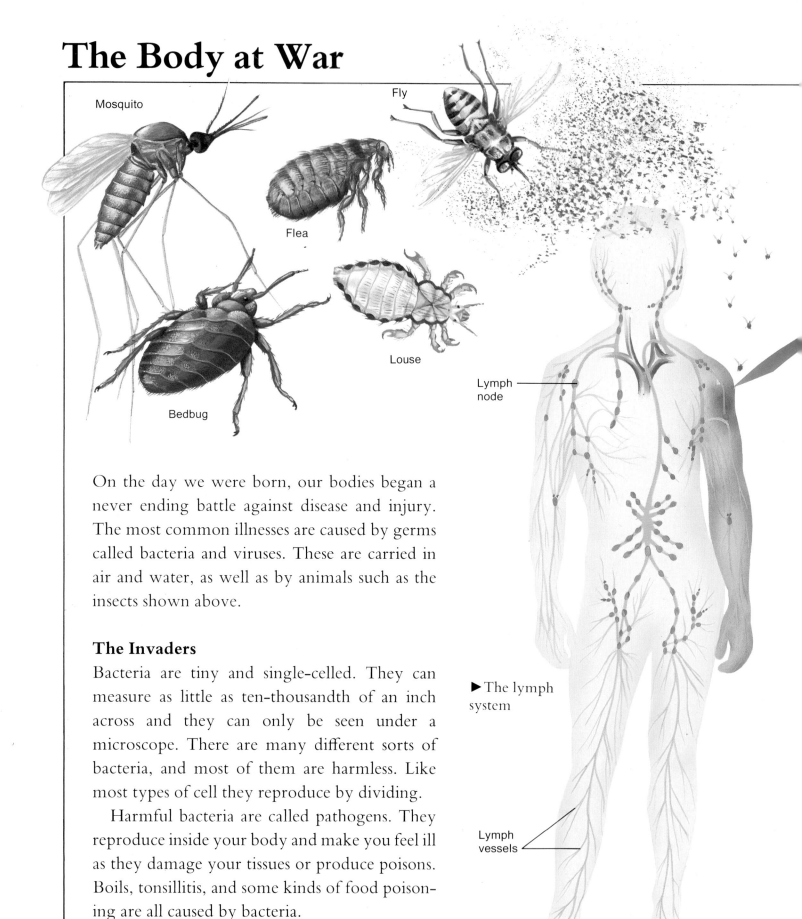

Mosquito

Fly

Flea

Louse

Bedbug

The lymph system

Lymph node

Lymph vessels

On the day we were born, our bodies began a never ending battle against disease and injury. The most common illnesses are caused by germs called bacteria and viruses. These are carried in air and water, as well as by animals such as the insects shown above.

The Invaders

Bacteria are tiny and single-celled. They can measure as little as ten-thousandth of an inch across and they can only be seen under a microscope. There are many different sorts of bacteria, and most of them are harmless. Like most types of cell they reproduce by dividing.

Harmful bacteria are called pathogens. They reproduce inside your body and make you feel ill as they damage your tissues or produce poisons. Boils, tonsillitis, and some kinds of food poisoning are all caused by bacteria.

Viruses are even smaller than bacteria. They

The lymph system forms the body's main attack force and protects it from the illnesses caused by germs (bacteria and viruses).

At intervals along the lymph vessels are small swellings called nodes. This is where special white blood cells called lympho-cytes are made. Lymphocytes make disease-fighting antibodies, which are released into the blood when germs invade.

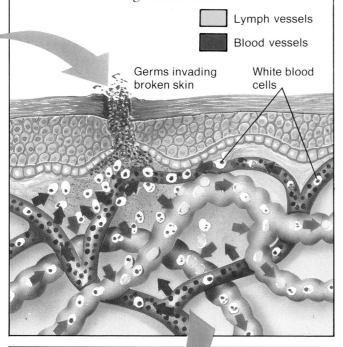

Lymph vessels

Blood vessels

Germs invading broken skin

White blood cells

There are several kinds of white blood cell in your blood. Ones called phagocytes destroy bacteria by surrounding and eating them. Pus forms if the bacteria kill the phagocytes.

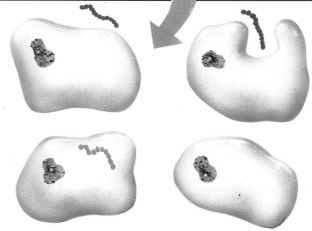

can only grow inside living cells, and as they do this they destroy the cells. There are hundreds of different viruses, and the diseases they cause include flu, measles, and chicken pox.

Illnesses caused by bacteria and viruses are infectious — they can be passed on from one person to another.

Defense and Attack

Your skin is your first line of defense. However, if this is broken, germs can get inside you. They can also get inside you in the air you breathe, or in the food and water you swallow.

Your body's main attack force is called the lymph system. Like the blood system, it is a set of vessels which carry liquid around the body. The liquid is called lymph.

The Lymph System

Lymph contains special white blood cells called lymphocytes. These can make sub-stances called antibodies, which fight germs and cope with poisons.

We are all born with some antibodies, and they increase after we come in contact with a disease. This is because once the body has produced an antibody to a certain disease, it can make the same antibody again very quickly if the same bacteria or virus strikes a second time. This is why, when we've had an illness such as measles or chicken pox once, we usually become immune to it, or pro-tected against it. It is for this reason that we are vaccinated against certain diseases.

The Breath of Life

In order to make energy to help the body grow and keep going, cells need a gas called oxygen in addition to the nutrients they get from the food you eat. If they are starved of either oxygen or nutrients, cells run out of energy and eventually die.

Breathing in, Breathing out

You take oxygen gas into your lungs from the air when you breathe in. The oxygen passes into your blood and is then carried to the body cells. Blood also carries nutrients to all the cells in the body.

Inside each cell, the oxygen and nutrients are "burned" to make energy. During this process, water and a gas called carbon dioxide are produced as waste materials. This waste is carried back to your lungs by your blood, to leave your body when you breathe out.

Where are the Lungs?

You have two lungs, one in each side of your chest, enclosed by an airtight box. Your ribs and the muscles that join them form the box, together with a tough sheet of muscle called the diaphragm.

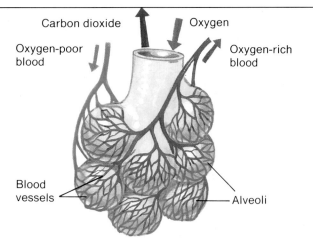

Inside the lungs are tiny air sacs called alveoli, surrounded by capillaries. The walls of the alveoli and capillaries are so thin that oxygen and carbon dioxide can pass through them.

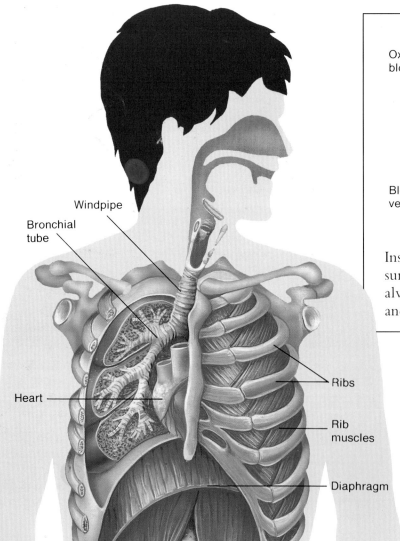

◄Your lungs fill with air when you breathe in, and empty when you breathe out. They go up and down rather like balloons, but they aren't just hollow bags. They are spongy organs made up of tightly packed tissue, nerves, and blood vessels.

Your windpipe branches into two bronchial tubes, one for each lung. Inside the lungs the tubes divide again and again, becoming smaller and smaller until they end in tiny air sacs called alveoli.

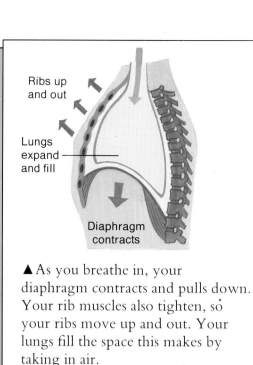

Ribs up
and out

Lungs
expand
and fill

Diaphragm
contracts

▼Your diaphragm relaxes and arches up to make you breathe out. Your rib muscles relax and your ribs move down and in. This forces some of the air out of your lungs.

Ribs down
and in

Lungs
contract
and
empty

Diaphragm
relaxes

▲As you breathe in, your diaphragm contracts and pulls down. Your rib muscles also tighten, so your ribs move up and out. Your lungs fill the space this makes by taking in air.

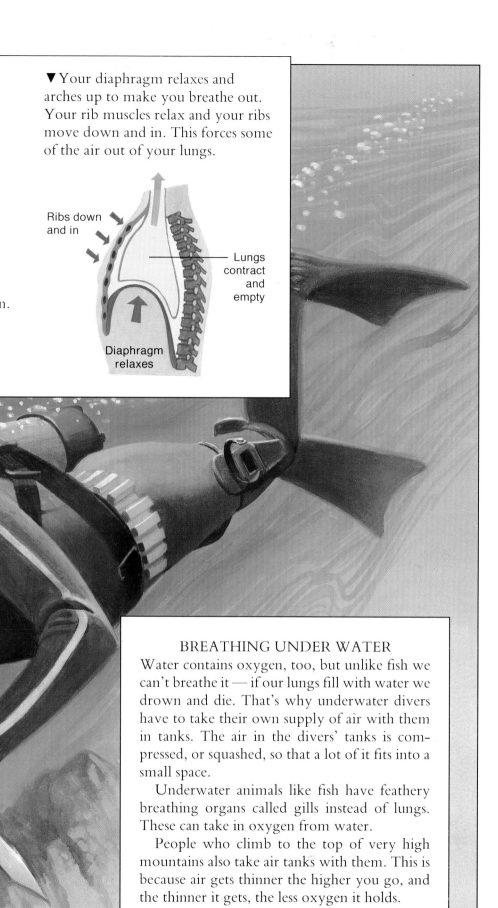

BREATHING UNDER WATER

Water contains oxygen, too, but unlike fish we can't breathe it — if our lungs fill with water we drown and die. That's why underwater divers have to take their own supply of air with them in tanks. The air in the divers' tanks is compressed, or squashed, so that a lot of it fits into a small space.

Underwater animals like fish have feathery breathing organs called gills instead of lungs. These can take in oxygen from water.

People who climb to the top of very high mountains also take air tanks with them. This is because air gets thinner the higher you go, and the thinner it gets, the less oxygen it holds.

Brain Power

The brain is the body's control center. It keeps the body working smoothly, and it looks after thoughts, feelings, and memory.

Different Parts, Different Jobs

Different parts of the brain have different jobs to do. The largest part is called the cerebrum, or forebrain. It looks like a huge half walnut. The cerebrum's main job is to sort out and respond to messages sent to it from the senses. It also stores information, as memory, and it thinks.

Messages from the senses are managed by the cerebrum's sensory area, while the motor area controls the muscles. Thinking, memory, and speech are managed by the parts known as the association areas.

The cerebellum, or hindbrain, is below the cerebrum. It works with the cerebrum's motor area to ensure that the muscles function smoothly.

The Nervous System

The brain is linked to the rest of the body by nerves. A large bundle of nerves runs from the brain down the back, inside the vertebrae that make up the spine. It is called the spinal cord and it is an extension of the brain. Smaller nerves run from the spinal cord to the rest of the body.

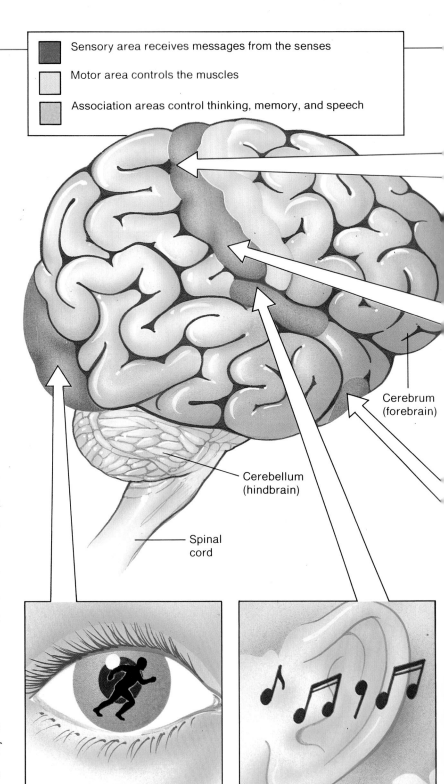

- Sensory area receives messages from the senses
- Motor area controls the muscles
- Association areas control thinking, memory, and speech

Cerebrum (forebrain)

Cerebellum (hindbrain)

Spinal cord

▲ The rear of the cerebrum receives messages from the eyes via the optic nerve, and turns the messages into pictures in your mind.

▲ The central area receives messages from the ears via the auditory nerve, and passes them on to be analyzed by the association areas.

16

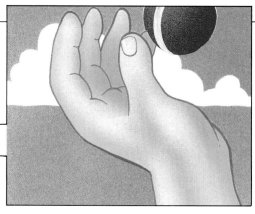

▲ Different parts of the touch-and-pain area control different parts of the body — from fingers to toes.

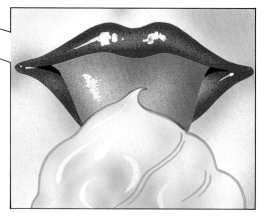

▲ The taste area. Our area of taste is well developed, but few people learn how to use it to the full.

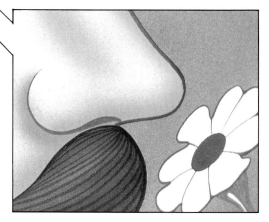

▲ The part of the brain that controls smell is at the front of the cerebrum. Humans have a less developed sense of smell than other animals, and this area of the brain is small.

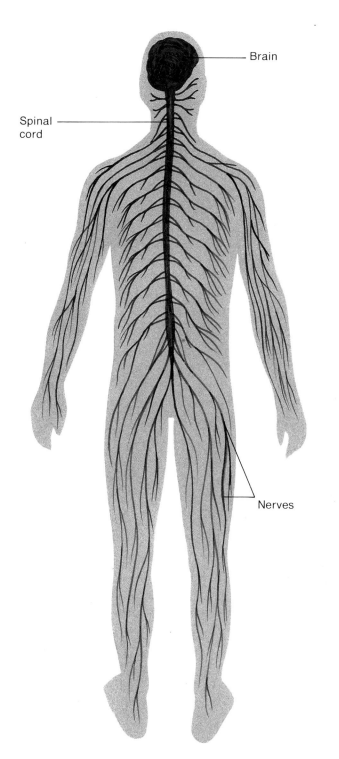

Brain

Spinal cord

Nerves

▲ The brain and spinal cord are known as the central nervous system. The smaller nerves that come out of the brain and spinal cord are called the peripheral nervous system. Nerves reach every part of the body, even the bones.

17

The Body's Hotlines

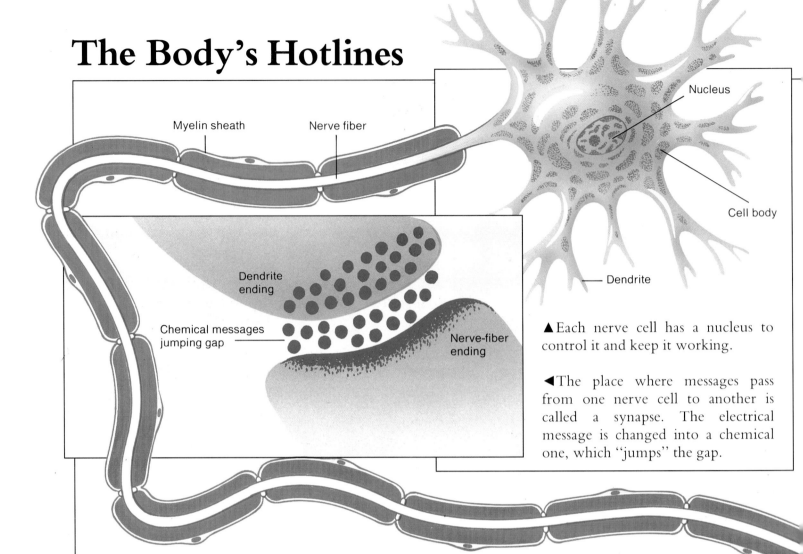

Myelin sheath
Nerve fiber
Nucleus
Cell body
Dendrite

Dendrite ending
Chemical messages jumping gap
Nerve-fiber ending

▲Each nerve cell has a nucleus to control it and keep it working.

◄The place where messages pass from one nerve cell to another is called a synapse. The electrical message is changed into a chemical one, which "jumps" the gap.

Nerves work rather like telephone wires, carrying information to and from the brain in the form of tiny electrical currents. The brain and spinal cord — the central nervous system (CNS, for short) — act like the telephone exchange, sorting and redirecting messages from the nerves.

Inside a Nerve

All nerves are bundles of thousands of tiny cells. Each nerve cell has a body with lots of branching arms called dendrites, and a long tail called a nerve fiber.

The dendrites pick up messages and carry them to the cell body, then the messages continue along the nerve fiber to the dendrites of another nerve cell. In this way information is passed from cell to cell until it reaches the correct body part.

Getting Messages Across

The ends of nerve cells never quite touch each other, and the electrical current is changed into a chemical message which "jumps" the gap. The place where messages pass from one nerve cell to another is called a synapse.

Many nerve fibers are wrapped in a fatty substance called myelin. This sheath, or covering, helps to direct the electrical messages and to keep them moving quickly.

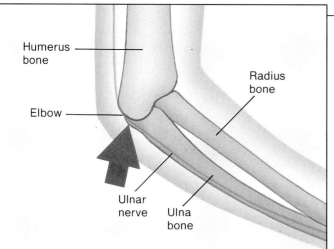

Humerus bone

Radius bone

Elbow

Ulnar nerve

Ulna bone

Although you may talk about bumping your funny bone, there's really no such bone in your body! The tingling you feel when you bump your elbow is actually the ulnar nerve being pinched against the ulnar bone. This makes the nerve send "wrong" messages to the brain — you feel as though your whole arm is tingling, even though you've only banged your elbow.

Sorting Messages

When a nerve receives a message from the body, it passes the information along to the CNS, where it is sorted and analyzed. If the brain decides to act on the information, the CNS then sends a new message back along other nerves, telling the body what to do.

Amazingly, all this takes a fraction of a second! As you lift a spoon to your mouth, for instance, millions of messages about the position, size, and angle of the spoon are being sent to your brain. Your brain analyzes the information at lightning speed and immediately sends out new messages to your muscles to adjust the movements of your arm, hand, and mouth.

We do some things without thinking about them. If we touch something very hot, for example, our hands jerk away. This kind of response is called a reflex action. It's when the body reacts without waiting for a message from the brain. The message travels from nerve-endings in the fingers to the spinal cord, then straight out again to the muscles, bypassing the brain.

▼ There are two basic kinds of nerve cell. Sensory nerve cells carry messages from the skin and senses to the CNS. Motor nerve cells carry messages back from the CNS to the muscles.

The illustration below shows how the end of the nerve fiber of a motor nerve cell is buried in the muscle tissue, so the electrical messages from the brain travel directly into the muscle.

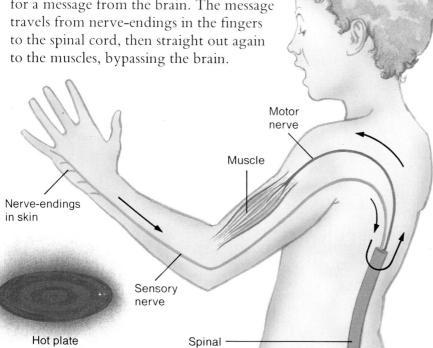

Motor nerve

Muscle

Nerve-endings in skin

Sensory nerve

Hot plate

Spinal cord

How Many Senses?

You have five main senses — sight, hearing, touch, taste, and smell. They are important because they keep your brain informed about the world outside your body.

All the information that the brain gets from the senses is collected by special cells called sensory receptors. These are often clustered together in sense organs such as the nose, mouth, eyes, or ears. None of these receptors can actually smell, taste, see, or hear. They merely collect information and then send messages via the nerves to the brain, which analyzes everything so it can tell us what the information means and what to do about it.

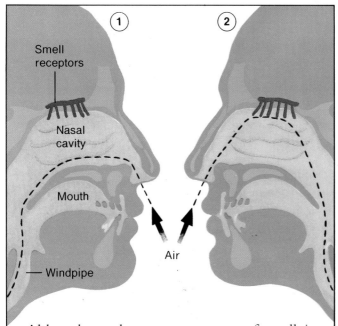

Although we have a poor sense of smell in comparison to other animals, our brain can tell the difference between several thousand smells. When we breathe in normally (1), only a small number of scent molecules dissolve in mucus and reach the smell receptors. If we want to identify a particular smell, we sniff (2). This carries more scent particles higher up the nostrils, directly onto the receptors.

Your Sense of Smell

Your smell receptors are in the upper half of your nose, in a space called the nasal cavity.

Smell receptors are affected by scent particles — tiny chemical units called molecules in the air you breathe. Each receptor cell has minute hairs which are covered with a sticky substance called mucus. When you breathe in, the scent particles in the air dissolve in the mucus. The smell receptors pick up the information and then pass it on to nerve cells, which carry it to the brain.

You may have noticed that food doesn't taste so good when you have a blocked nose. This is because when we eat or drink something, much of what we think is taste is really smell. Taste and smell work together because the nose and mouth are so closely connected.

OTHER SENSES
You have other senses beside the five main ones, including those of balance, hunger, and thirst. Your sense of pain is very important — it warns you when your body is hurt or in danger.

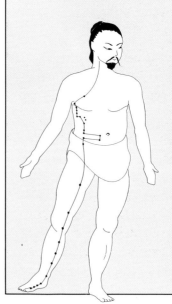

◄Acupuncture is an ancient Chinese form of medical treatment which is sometimes used instead of drugs to relieve pain and to manage illness. Very fine needles are inserted along the body's meridians — lines along which acupuncturists believe the body's life forces flow.

Your Sense of Taste

The groups of receptor cells on your tongue are called tastebuds, and they are positioned around the base of the tiny bumps that cover the surface of your tongue. Tastebuds are affected when certain chemicals in food dissolve in a digestive juice called saliva, which your mouth produces. Information about taste travels to your brain via nerves and is analyzed by a special area of the cerebrum.

There are only four basic tastes — bitter, sweet, sour, and salty. Different tastebuds in different parts of the tongue are sensitive to each one. The back of the tongue is particularly sensitive to bitter tastes, while the sides respond more to sour tastes. Tastebuds that are sensitive to sweet and salty tastes are grouped at the front of the tongue.

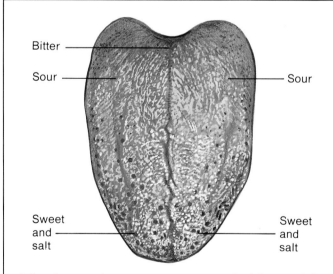

The four main tastes are sweet, salt, bitter, and sour, and you taste them with different parts of your tongue. You can check where the four tastes are on your tongue by dabbing it with a little salt, sugar, coffee grounds (bitter), and lemon juice (sour).

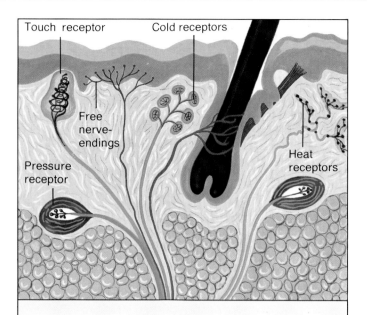

Your skin is a huge sense organ with thousands of sensory receptors. Skin receptors are not only sensitive to touch and texture — telling you whether something is smooth or furry, for example. There are also receptors that respond to heat, and ones that respond to cold. Yet others tell you when something is putting pressure on your skin.

Some skin receptors are sensitive to all four. They are called free nerve endings and they are thought to send out pain signals if messages from touch, heat, cold, or pressure receptors are too strong. There are free nerve endings wrapped around the hairs in your skin, sensitive to each hair's slightest movement.

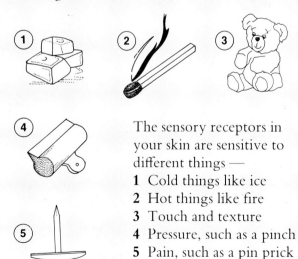

The sensory receptors in your skin are sensitive to different things —
1 Cold things like ice
2 Hot things like fire
3 Touch and texture
4 Pressure, such as a pinch
5 Pain, such as a pin prick

Skin Deep

Skin covers your body in a pastry-thin layer, in most parts around a twelfth-inch (0.2 cm) thick, but about a tenth-inch (0.25 cm) thick on the soles of your feet and the palms of your hands. It is waterproof and stretchy, and it protects you from the outside world by helping to keep out harmful things like dirt and germs.

Peeling Back the Layers

Skin has two main layers. The protective outer layer is called the epidermis. The skin you can see on your body is the top of the epidermis, which is made of dead cells. New cells are made at the bottom of the epidermis and gradually push their way upward.

The inner layer of the skin is called the dermis. The sensory receptors for touch, heat, cold, pressure, and pain are here, as well as the nerve endings that pick up information and carry it to the brain. The dermis is also where sweat is made and hair grows.

Looking at Hair

Skin feels smooth, but under a microscope it looks like a jagged mountain range with huge pits sprouting hair. These pits are called follicles, and they make hair straight or curly. Straight hair grows from a round follicle, wavy hair grows from an oval-shaped one, and very curly hair grows from a flat one.

The number of hairs you have on your head depends on the color of your hair. Most blondes have about 140,000 head hairs. Redheads average 90,000. People with black or brown hair come somewhere in the middle, with about 110,000 hairs.

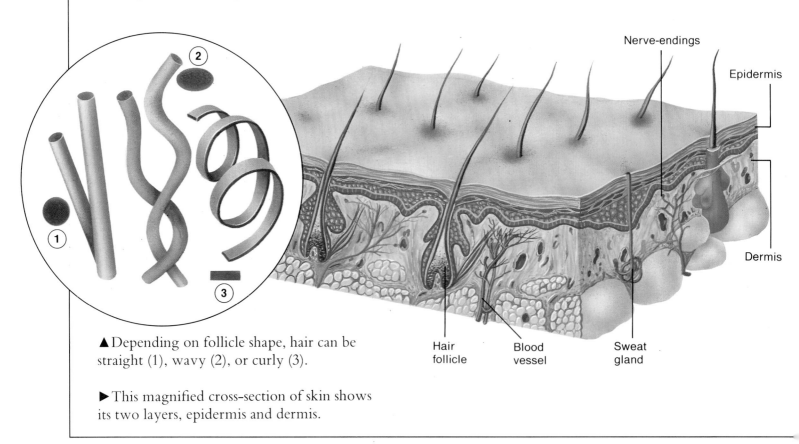

▲ Depending on follicle shape, hair can be straight (1), wavy (2), or curly (3).

▶ This magnified cross-section of skin shows its two layers, epidermis and dermis.

WHEN YOU ARE COLD

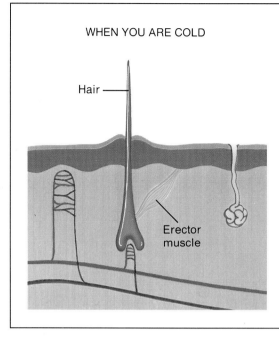

Hair

Erector muscle

◄Each hair has a tiny erector muscle. When you are cold, these muscles contract to make the hairs stand up, trapping warm air between them and giving you goosebumps.

►In hot weather, the tiny blood vessels in your skin widen and carry more warm blood to the surface, where the outside air can cool it. The hairs lie flat, so warm air isn't trapped by them.

WHEN YOU ARE HOT

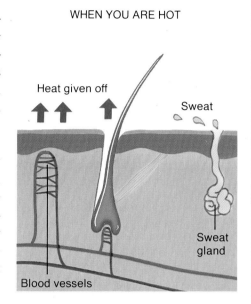

Heat given off

Sweat

Sweat gland

Blood vessels

►Nails grow at a rate of about a tenth of an inch (0.25 cm) a month. Like hair, they are made of dead cells and have no feeling except at the root, where new nail grows — that's why cutting them doesn't hurt. The root is the bottom of the nail, under the cuticle. Nail and hair are made of a tough material called keratin.

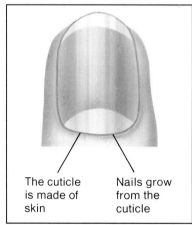

The cuticle is made of skin

Nails grow from the cuticle

►Your fingerprints are quite unlike anyone else's. The ridges of skin on the fingertips form a pattern, and everyone's pattern is different. People's palm prints are also different. You can check this by making ink prints of your hands and comparing them with a friend's hand prints.

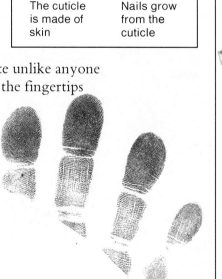

Hands are among the body's most sensitive parts, with millions of nerve endings. The fingertips are the most sensitive parts of the hand.

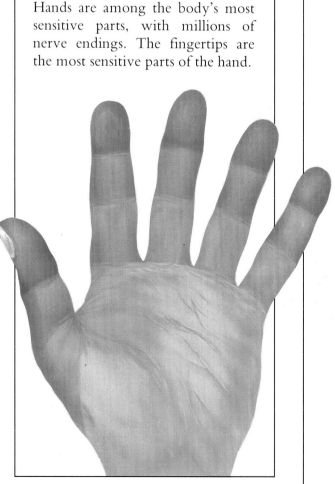

Seeing is Believing

Our eyes weigh only a quarter-ounce (7 grams) each and measure just $\frac{3}{4}$-inch (2 cm) across. Yet they contain more than 130 million special cells which are sensitive to light. With the help of the brain, these cells allow us to see the color, size, and shape of the things around us, as well as telling us how far away objects are and when they move.

Getting Things in Focus

Covering the front of each eye is a delicate see-through layer called the cornea. Light entering the eye is mainly focused by the cornea, but also by the pupil and lens behind it. These can change shape to finetune the focusing.

The back of the eye has a special lining called the retina which contains the eye's light-sensitive cells. Each one is joined by tiny nerves to the optic nerve, which leads to the brain.

There are no light-sensitive cells at the point where the optic nerve enters the eye. This point is called the blind spot.

Protecting and Cleaning

Pupils are the black centers to the eyes. They're holes which let in light and they are between the cornea and the lens. The pupils can vary in size to control the amount of light entering the eye. This helps to protect the retina from too much light, as well as sharpening the image.

Eyelids and eyelashes stop bits of dirt getting in the eyes. Tears keep them moist and wash them clean — blinking spreads tears over the eyes. The average person blinks his or her eyelids millions of times a year!

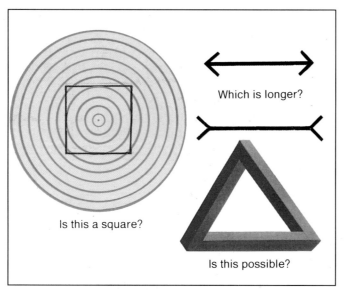

Which is longer?

Is this a square?

Is this possible?

◄ Even if your eyesight is good, you can't always believe what you see. Cover your left eye and look at the dot with your right. Now hold the book at arm's length away from you. Move it nearer slowly. The dot seems to disappear when light from it falls on the blind spot inside your eye.

▼ The iris is the colored ring around the pupil of the eye. Muscles in the iris contract to make the pupil close up, so that it lets in less light. They relax to let the pupil open up in dim light, so you can see better.

BRIGHT LIGHT

DIM LIGHT

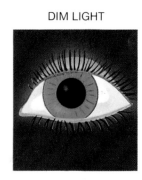

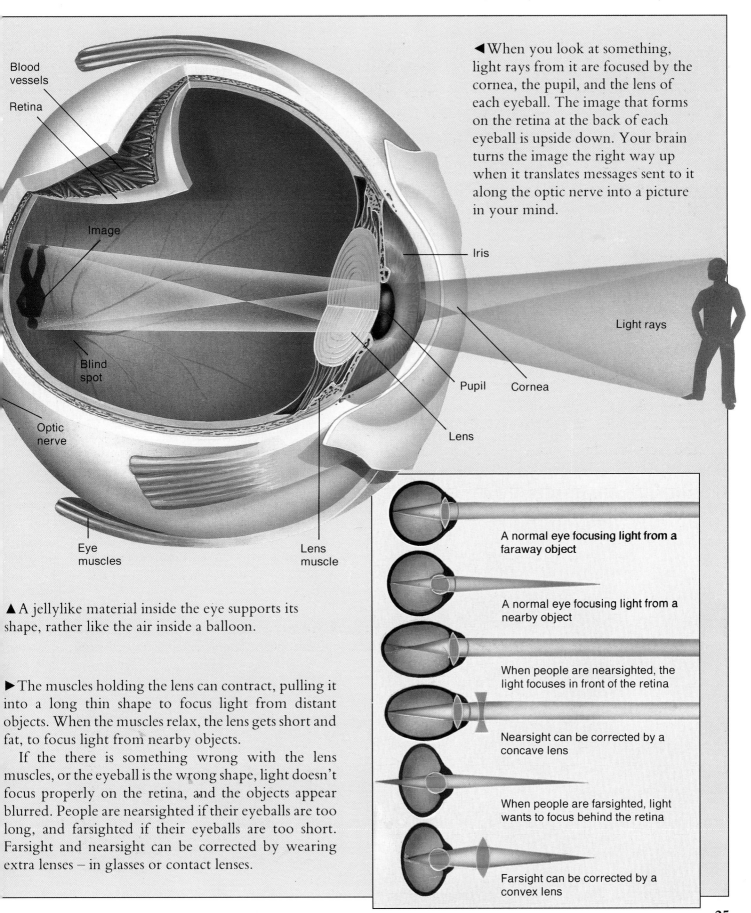

Blood vessels

Retina

Image

Blind spot

Optic nerve

Eye muscles

Lens muscle

◄ When you look at something, light rays from it are focused by the cornea, the pupil, and the lens of each eyeball. The image that forms on the retina at the back of each eyeball is upside down. Your brain turns the image the right way up when it translates messages sent to it along the optic nerve into a picture in your mind.

Iris

Light rays

Pupil   Cornea

Lens

▲ A jellylike material inside the eye supports its shape, rather like the air inside a balloon.

► The muscles holding the lens can contract, pulling it into a long thin shape to focus light from distant objects. When the muscles relax, the lens gets short and fat, to focus light from nearby objects.

If the there is something wrong with the lens muscles, or the eyeball is the wrong shape, light doesn't focus properly on the retina, and the objects appear blurred. People are nearsighted if their eyeballs are too long, and farsighted if their eyeballs are too short. Farsight and nearsight can be corrected by wearing extra lenses – in glasses or contact lenses.

A normal eye focusing light from a faraway object

A normal eye focusing light from a nearby object

When people are nearsighted, the light focuses in front of the retina

Nearsight can be corrected by a concave lens

When people are farsighted, light wants to focus behind the retina

Farsight can be corrected by a convex lens

Hearing and Balance

We usually think of our ears merely as things to hear with. The parts we can see are called the outer ear. They are designed to collect sounds and funnel them into the inner parts of the ear. These are hidden inside our heads and one of their most important jobs is helping us to keep our balance.

Our Sense of Balance

Three loops called semicircular canals give us our sense of balance. They are in the inner ear, on top of a snail-shaped tube which is called the cochlea.

The canals are filled with liquid and lined with tiny hairs, which are in turn connected to nerve endings.

Staying Upright

When you move, the liquid inside the semicircular canals swirls around. This bends the hairs in the canals, making them push against their nerve endings. Messages then travel to the auditory nerve and on to the brain, telling it what you are doing.

You feel dizzy after you spin around and around because the liquid in your ears is still swirling about when you stop, and your brain can't tell where you're going!

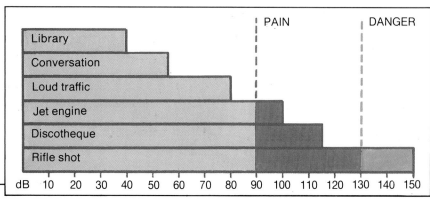

	PAIN	DANGER
Library		
Conversation		
Loud traffic		
Jet engine		
Discotheque		
Rifle shot		
dB 10 20 30 40 50 60 70 80 90 100 110 120 130 140 150		

◄Noise is measured in units called decibels (dB). Loud noises can damage your ears — a rifle shot could deafen you for a while, for example. But the length of time a sound lasts is also important. A noise which isn't as loud as a rifle shot, but which goes on for longer, could be more damaging.

▶ Sound vibrations travel from the outer ear to the inner ear through three tiny bones. These are called the hammer, anvil, and stirrup because of their shape.

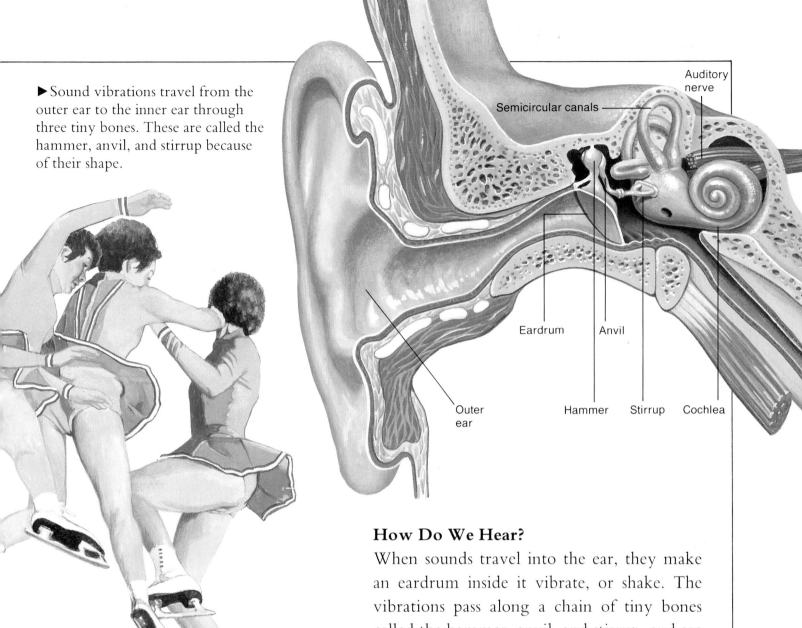

▲ The inner ear is the body's main organ of balance, but the brain also receives messages from nerve endings in the neck, back, leg, and foot muscles.

The brain sifts all this information and sends messages back to the muscles, allowing us to perform incredible feats of balance such as ice-skating or gymnastics.

How Do We Hear?

When sounds travel into the ear, they make an eardrum inside it vibrate, or shake. The vibrations pass along a chain of tiny bones called the hammer, anvil, and stirrup, and are made louder before passing into the cochlea.

The vibrations are then picked up by nerve-endings inside the cochlea, and changed into messages to send to the brain.

Harmful Noises

Loud noises make the eardrum tighten, pulling the stirrup bone away from the cochlea in order to protect the inner ear. Very loud noises can tear the eardrum and cause deafness. Fortunately, small tears usually heal up over a period of time.

What Happens to Food?

Everything you eat has to be chopped up and broken down before the nutrients or goodness in it can be taken into your blood and used by your body cells to make energy. This chopping up and breaking down takes place in your digestive system, or gut.

Your digestive system is a long tube which begins at your mouth and ends at your anus. In adults it is about 30 feet (9 m) long! Food takes 10 to 20 hours to pass through it.

The Journey Begins

Digestion starts with your first bite. In your mouth, the food is chopped up and chewed by your teeth, and mixed with a digestive juice called saliva. Your tongue pushes and kneads the food into a ball. This ball of food is then pushed down a short tube called the esophagus to your stomach.

Inside Your Stomach

Food stays inside your stomach for about 3 hours. It's mixed with more digestive juices which are produced in the stomach walls. Acid in the digestive juices helps to kill any bacteria in the food.

Your stomach wall contracts to churn and knead the food. Together with the digestive juices, it breaks the food down until it turns into a thick creamy soup.

Onward and Downward

The food leaves your stomach a little at a time and goes into your small intestine. This is where most of the digestion takes place.

Your small intestine is coiled neatly inside your abdomen, or belly, and it's the longest part of your digestive system — in adults it's about 20 feet (6 m) long.

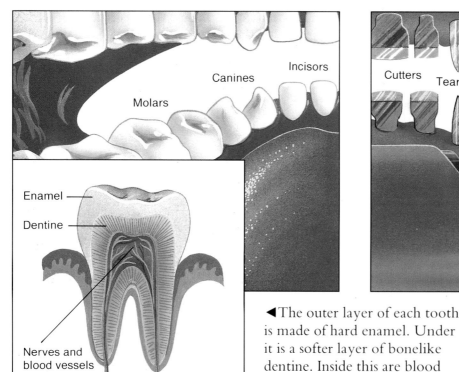

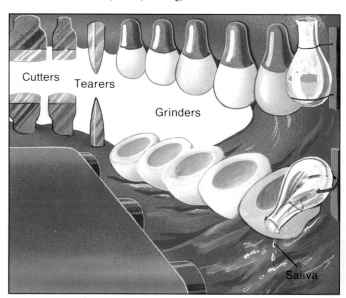

◄ The outer layer of each tooth is made of hard enamel. Under it is a softer layer of bonelike dentine. Inside this are blood vessels and nerves.

▲ Because we eat such a variety of food we have three different types of tooth. Each does a different job — incisors cut, canines tear, and molars grind.

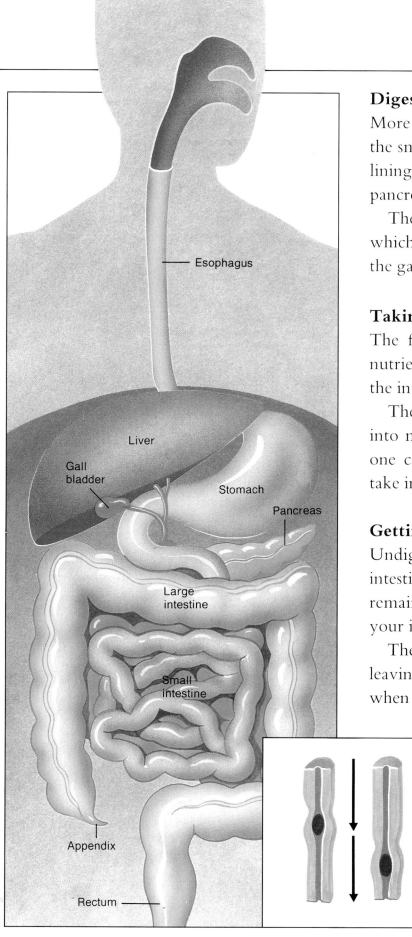

Esophagus

Liver

Gall bladder

Stomach

Pancreas

Large intestine

Small intestine

Appendix

Rectum

Digestive Juice Factories

More digestive juices are added to the food in the small intestine. The juices are made in the lining of the intestine walls, and by the pancreas and liver.

The liver makes a green liquid called bile which helps to break down fat. Bile is stored in the gall bladder.

Taking in Nutrients

The food is broken down until it contains nutrients that are small enough to pass through the intestine wall.

The lining of the small intestine is folded into millions of tiny fingers called villi. Each one contains a network of capillaries which take in nutrients from the digested food.

Getting Rid of Waste

Undigested food continues on to the large intestine, where water is taken up from it. The remaining waste travels on to the last part of your intestine — the rectum.

The waste is stored here for a while before leaving your body as feces through your anus when you go to the toilet.

◄Food and drink would travel down your esophagus even if you ate upside down! This is because muscles in the esophagus wall contract to squeeze the food along, rather like the toothpaste in a tube. This squeezing process is called peristalsis.

When you swallow food, a flap called the epiglottis closes over the top of your windpipe so that the food doesn't go down it.

War on Waste

Our body cells "burn" nutrients and oxygen to make energy to live and grow, in much the same way that wood and other materials are burned to produce another sort of energy — heat. But just as fires produce waste gases and ash, so the "burning" that takes place in our body cells also creates waste materials. These must be removed, or they would poison us.

The Kidneys

The removal of these waste materials is known as excretion, and the body's main organs of excretion are the kidneys. The lungs, the liver, and the sweat glands in the skin also help the body to remove waste materials.

You have two kidneys, positioned in the small of your back, one on either side of your backbone. They look like large reddish-brown beans. Each one is roughly the size of your clenched fist.

Cleaning the Blood

Kidneys clean the blood by filtering out waste materials and straining off any water the body doesn't need. This liquid waste is called urine. It is stored in your bladder and leaves your body when you go to the toilet. The kidneys are connected to the bladder by long tubes called ureters.

Two main blood vessels run to and from the kidneys. Unfiltered blood is brought from the body via the renal artery. When the blood has been cleaned it goes back to the body via the renal vein.

► ▼Inside a kidney, waste materials are filtered out of the blood in the outer layer, the cortex. Some water is put back into the blood in the inner layer, the medulla, and urine flows away down the ureter.

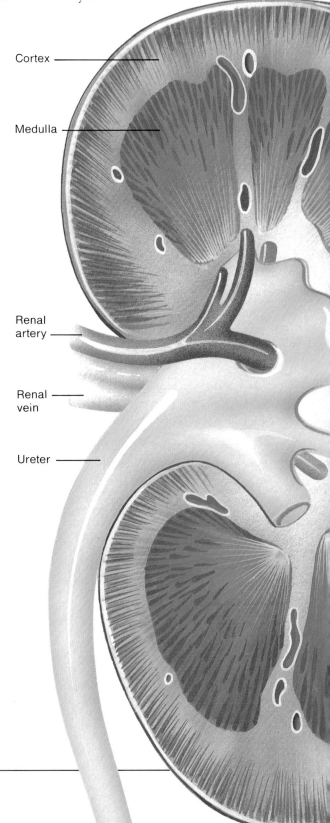

Cortex

Medulla

Renal artery

Renal vein

Ureter

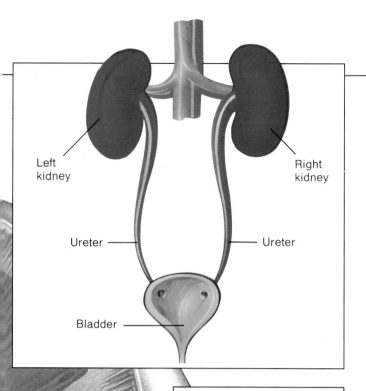

Left kidney

Right kidney

Ureter — Ureter

Bladder

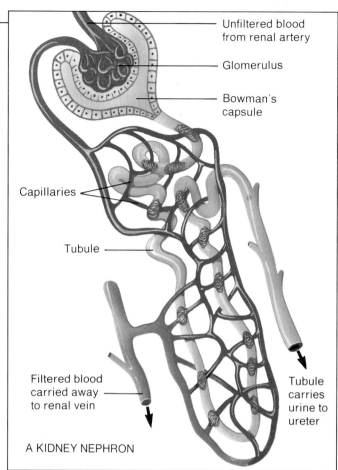

Unfiltered blood from renal artery

Glomerulus

Bowman's capsule

Capillaries

Tubule

Filtered blood carried away to renal vein

Tubule carries urine to ureter

A KIDNEY NEPHRON

▶The millions of tiny filtering units inside the kidneys are called nephrons. The renal artery brings unfiltered blood to the kidneys. It branches into over a million capillaries inside each kidney. Each capillary is twisted into a knot called the glomerulus which is enclosed by a structure called a Bowman's capsule.

Blood is cleaned as it filters through the capsule and the tubule attached to it. Clean blood passes back into capillaries which join up into the renal vein.

Urine continues down the tubule, which joins up with other tubules to form the ureter leading to the bladder.

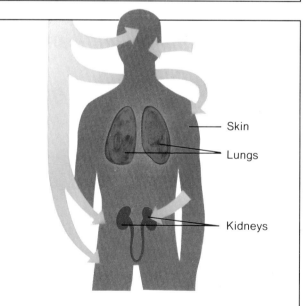

Skin

Lungs

Kidneys

We lose around 3 quarts (3 liters) of water a day through our skin as sweat, and in our breath and urine. We also get rid of extra salt in sweat, and we expel waste carbon dioxide gas when we breathe out.

New Life Begins

A baby begins its life when a sperm cell from its father enters an ovum, or egg cell, from its mother. This moment is called fertilization or conception.

The sperm and egg cells join to make a new cell, which starts to grow and divide. It does this over and over again to make the millions of cells that will form the different parts of the baby's body — from heart, lungs, and brain, to skin, hair, and fingernails.

The Journey of Life

Sperm cells are made in a man's two testes. Egg cells are stored in a woman's two ovaries. Each month, one egg cell ripens and passes into a fallopian tube. It then moves down toward the uterus, or womb.

When a couple make love, the man's penis becomes stiff and is placed inside the woman's vagina. About 300 million tiny sperm squirt out of the penis into the vagina.

▼Inside a man, sperm cells are made inside each testis and stored in a coiled tube called the epididymus. When a man makes love, the sperm travel along the vas deferens and urethra to the penis.

Each sperm cell has a tail and a head which contains its nucleus. The sperm swim up the vagina and into the womb by waving their tails. They continue on upward toward the egg cell in the fallopian tube.

Around 100 sperm cells may reach the egg cell, but only one can enter and fertilize it.

Growing and Dividing

After fertilization, the new cell passes down the fallopian tube toward the womb, where it becomes fixed in the womb wall. This is where it will stay over the next 8 to 9 months while it grows into a baby.

The baby is joined to its mother by the umbilical cord and the placenta. Blood in the umbilical cord carries food and oxygen from the mother to the baby, and takes waste away. The placenta forms where the first ball of cells becomes fixed to the womb wall. It is where the baby's and mother's blood meet.

▼Inside a woman, egg cells are stored inside the ovaries. One egg is released each month — one month by one ovary and the next by the other. The egg cells travel down the fallopian tubes to the womb.

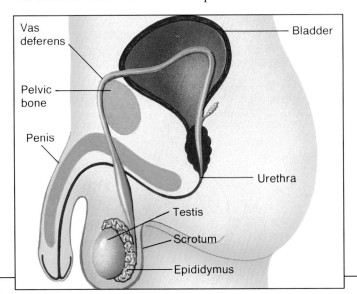

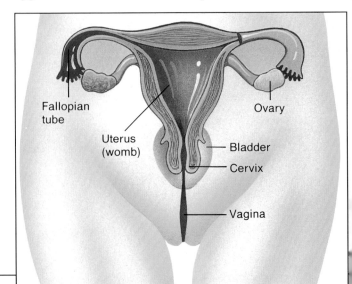

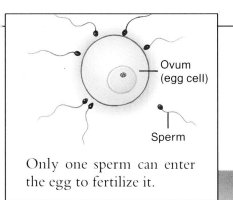

Ovum (egg cell)

Sperm

Only one sperm can enter the egg to fertilize it.

Over a few days, the new cell divides several times to make a ball of cells.

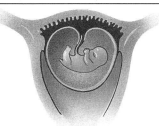

By 12 weeks the fetus, or growing baby, is about 3 inches (7.5 cm) long.

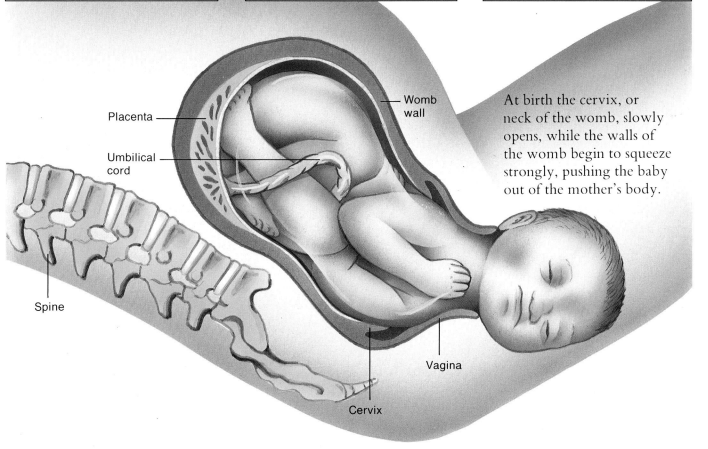

Placenta

Umbilical cord

Spine

Womb wall

Cervix

Vagina

At birth the cervix, or neck of the womb, slowly opens, while the walls of the womb begin to squeeze strongly, pushing the baby out of the mother's body.

By 18 weeks, the fetus is 9 inches (23 cm) long. Its main organs were formed by 12 weeks.

By 26 weeks, the fetus is about 14 inches (36 cm) long. For some time now it has been moving around.

At about 38 weeks, the baby is ready to leave its mother's body and be born.

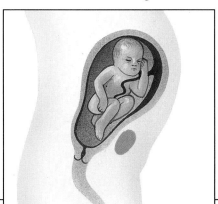

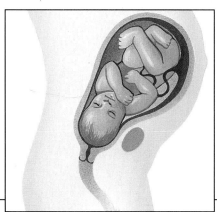

Growing Up and Growing Old

As babies grow into children and children grow into adults, many changes take place in their bodies. They grow taller, of course, and their bodies change shape.

Becoming an Adult

The time when someone starts changing from a child into an adult is called puberty. For girls, puberty usually begins between the ages of 10 and 14 years. Boys are usually 12 to 15 years old.

The main changes are the ones that prepare the body for having children. A boy's testes begin to produce sperm cells, and a girl's ovaries to make egg cells.

One egg cell is released each month. If it isn't fertilized by a sperm cell, the egg is shed from the girl's body through her vagina, together with the womb lining and some blood. This monthly bleeding is called menstruation or having a period.

Later Years

Our bodies are fully formed by the time we are about 20, then we slowly start to age. Gradually, our muscles become weaker and we can't move so fast. Bones become harder and break more easily, and joints become stiffer. Skin loses its stretchiness and sags, and hair turns white.

The main reason why our bodies start to wear out as we get older is that the cells take longer to reproduce themselves. This means that it takes longer to repair and replace damaged parts of the body.

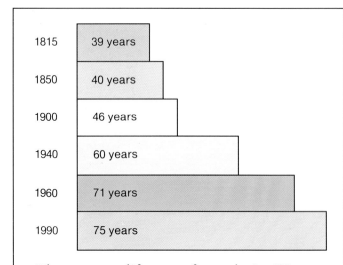

1815	39 years
1850	40 years
1900	46 years
1940	60 years
1960	71 years
1990	75 years

The average lifespan of people in Western countries, 1815–1990. Because of medical discoveries and improvements in living conditions, people now live longer than ever before.

Age 8

Age 6

Age 4

► Our faces change as we grow older. Babies have much smaller chins and noses than adults. As we age, muscles become weaker and skin stretches and wrinkles.

Age 15

Age 40

Age 60

Chemicals in Control

Although the brain is the body's main control center, it is backed up by special groups of cells known as endocrine glands. These produce chemicals called hormones, which are carried around the body in the blood.

Hormones control all sorts of things, from the rate at which we grow, to the amount of salt and water in the blood, and the way we react to fear or anger. Some hormones work only on a particular organ, but others affect the whole body.

The Master Gland

The pituitary is one of the most important endocrine glands. It is called the master gland because some of its hormones actually control the other glands' hormone production rates.

The pituitary also makes hormones that govern the body's rate of growth, and the amount of water the kidneys remove from the blood. Other pituitary hormones start womb contractions when women have babies and make them produce breast milk afterward.

The pituitary is attached to the underside of the brain and linked to an area called the hypothalamus. This area of the brain helps to control the pituitary.

Throat Glands

The thyroid gland controls the rate at which the body cells convert food into energy, as well as the body's rate of growth and the way nerves work. Parathyroids help to manage the amount of calcium in bones and blood, and the way the muscles work.

▲ Breastfeeding is controlled by a hormone called prolactin, which is made by the pituitary gland.

The Pancreas and Adrenal Glands

The pancreas is positioned below the stomach. It makes digestive juices and it produces a hormone called insulin which controls the level of sugar in the blood.

People can become very ill if their sugar levels are too low or too high. Someone whose body doesn't produce enough insulin suffers from an illness called diabetes.

The adrenal glands are just above the kidneys. Some of their hormones control long-term reaction to stress, as well as instant response to danger. Others control salt and water levels in the blood.

The Testes and Ovaries

These glands govern the start of puberty in boys and girls, and their development into men and women. Hormones produced in the ovaries make a woman's breasts develop. In men, the growth of hair on the face and body is controlled by hormones produced in the testes.

Men's testes produce sperm cells, and women's ovaries, egg cells. The ovaries also control women's periods, and body changes during pregnancy and childbirth.

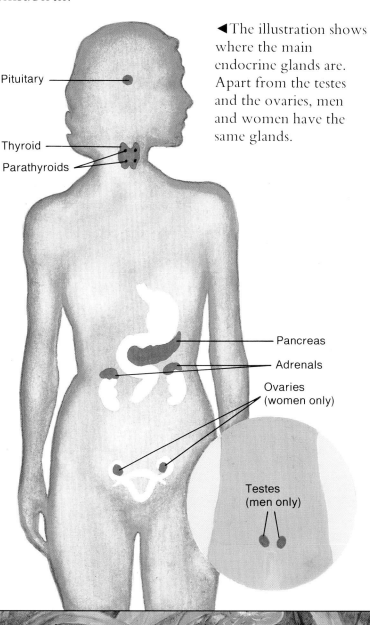

◄The illustration shows where the main endocrine glands are. Apart from the testes and the ovaries, men and women have the same glands.

Pituitary

Thyroid

Parathyroids

Pancreas

Adrenals

Ovaries (women only)

Testes (men only)

EMERGENCY HORMONES

Are you scared of spiders? When you're frightened or angry, your brain tells its hypothalmus area to send messages to your adrenal glands. These glands then increase the rate at which they produce two "emergency" hormones called adrenalin and noradrenalin.

These hormones increase the amount of sugar in your blood, and raise your heartbeat and breathing rates. This means that more blood gets around your body, carrying more oxygen. The emergency hormones also redirect blood from other parts of your body to your muscles. You are then ready for action — either to run, or to stand your ground and fight!

A Day in Your Life

Every day your body copes with hundreds of different situations, changing and adapting to keep you comfortable and well. The diagrams on these pages illustrate some of the ways your body responds to and deals with the different things that happen to you during the course of a day.

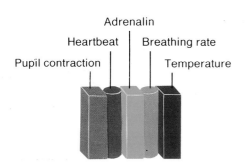

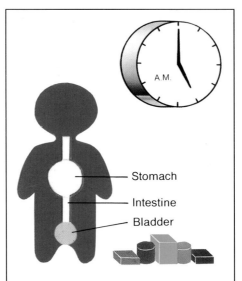

Your body relaxes while you sleep, and all your levels drop. Your pupils aren't contracted because your eyes are shut, blocking out light. Your bladder fills during the night.

Getting up makes your heartbeat, temperature, and breathing rates rise. Opening your eyes lets in light, making your pupils contract. You go to the toilet and empty your bladder.

You spend the evening quietly watching TV, and your levels drop to their lowest for the day. They will drop further when you go to bed and your body relaxes into sleep.

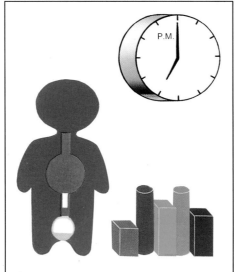

At dinner your levels are even lower. You fill your stomach, but some food from earlier in the day is still being digested in your intestine. Your bladder is filling up again.

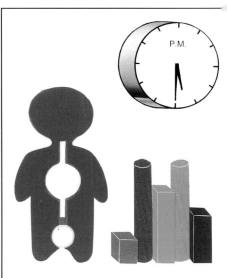

Home again. The emergency is over, so your levels return to normal. Your lunch is now being digested in your intestine. You go to the toilet and empty your bladder.

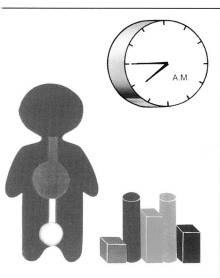

You sit down to eat breakfast, so your breathing rate slows down, although your temperature is still rising. Your stomach fills up as you eat. Digestion is beginning already.

Walking to school, your heartbeat and breathing rates increase to send more food and oxygen to your muscles. It's bright outside, so your pupils contract and get smaller.

You need less energy sitting at your desk inside the classroom, so your heartbeat and breathing rates drop. Your breakfast is now being digested in your small intestine.

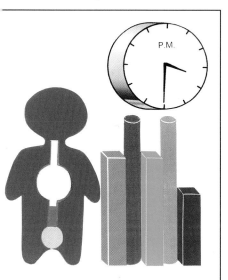

Emergency — you get cramp! Your heartbeat and adrenalin rates shoot up, and you breathe quickly and deeply. Your pupils open wide so you can see what is happening.

You go swimming after lunch. This uses up a lot of energy and makes your heartbeat and breathing rates rise sharply. Your lunch is moving down into your small intestine.

It's lunchtime and your stomach rumbles to tell you that you're hungry. All your levels are low when you sit down to eat. Your stomach fills up with food again as you eat.

Body Language

Watch a dog meeting other dogs and you will see it take up a number of different poses at different times – ears and nose down, tail between its legs, ears pricked, teeth bared, or tail up and wagging. Actions like these allow dogs to tell each other when they want to fight, to run away, or to make friends.

Humans have other ways of communicating – telling or showing each other our thoughts and feelings. We can talk, of course. But like dogs we also have a body language.

Speaking Without Words

Gestures are the movements we make with our face, head, arms, hands, and whole body to signal thoughts and feelings. Head and facial gestures can say a lot about how we feel – how often do you raise your eyebrows when you are surprised, for example, or nod your head when you say "yes"?

Whole body gestures – the way we stand or sit – can also communicate a lot. For example, confident people show they are sure of themselves by standing up straight.

Speaking With Words

Even newborn babies use sounds to communicate – they cry when they are hungry or tired. As they grow older, babies shape sounds into words and learn to talk. By the time most children are two they can use several hundred words. There are over 500,000 words in the English language, but most people only use a few thousand of them.

We don't only communicate through the actual words we use. The way we speak adds to what we are saying. We whisper a secret, for example, and we sometimes shout when we are angry. The words we stress and our tone of voice also alter our meaning.

FOREIGN LANGUAGES
People's gestures often mean different things in different countries. In some countries people shake hands when they greet each other, for example, but in other countries people rub noses to say hello or goodbye.

Underwater divers signal that everything is okay by making a circle with their forefinger and thumb. People in most countries recognize a raised thumb as also meaning okay.

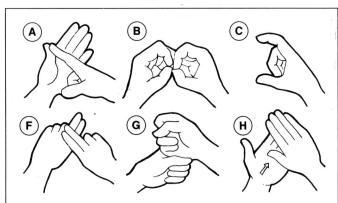

THE LANGUAGE OF HANDS
Although many people think of speech as our main way of communicating, we don't have to use spoken words. People who can't speak communicate by lip-reading or using signs. Some learn a language called signing in which hands and fingers are used to signal letters and words.

▲ ► Our body language shows how we feel. People who are tired and unhappy tend to hunch up and look smaller, like the person shown above. People who are exited and happy make big and confident gestures, like those of the athlete to the right, who has just won a race.

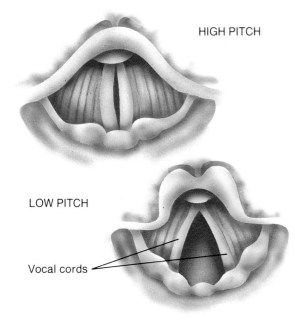

HIGH PITCH

LOW PITCH

Vocal cords

SHAPING SOUNDS INTO WORDS

We make sounds when air is forced through our vocal cords, making them vibrate.

The vocal cords are two rubbery bands of cartilage inside the larynx (or voice box). It's at the top of the windpipe and it shows up on the outside of the throat as a lump which is called the Adam's apple.

The muscles of the larynx can alter the shape of the cords to produce different sounds. The cords produce high-pitched sounds when they are stretched and close together, and low-pitched sounds when they are relaxed and far apart. The diagrams to the left show what your vocal cords would look like if you could see down your throat.

The harder the air is forced out, the louder the sounds you make. You use the muscles of your throat, mouth, and lips to form the sounds into words.

Modern Medicine

Bodies and internal organs such as the heart are not always as fit and healthy as they could be. Sometimes a baby is born with a part of its body that doesn't work as well as it should. And as we get older and our bodies start to wear out, organs sometimes stop working properly. Fortunately, doctors have developed ways to mend or replace a variety of body parts if they become damaged.

Giving Parts Away

Doctors usually need to give patients extra blood during operations, so a ready supply of blood is important to hospitals. Many people go to special centers to give some of their blood to help. These people are called donors.

Some people also promise to give away parts of their bodies if they have an accident and die. They hope that their healthy heart, for example, will be put into the body of someone with a damaged heart, saving that person's life.

Swapping Parts

When a doctor replaces a damaged organ with a healthy one from a donor, the operation is called a transplant. Nowadays the heart, liver, kidneys, and lungs can all be transplanted. And because the treatment for some types of cancer destroys the vital bone marrow where blood cells are made, bone marrow transplants are also very important.

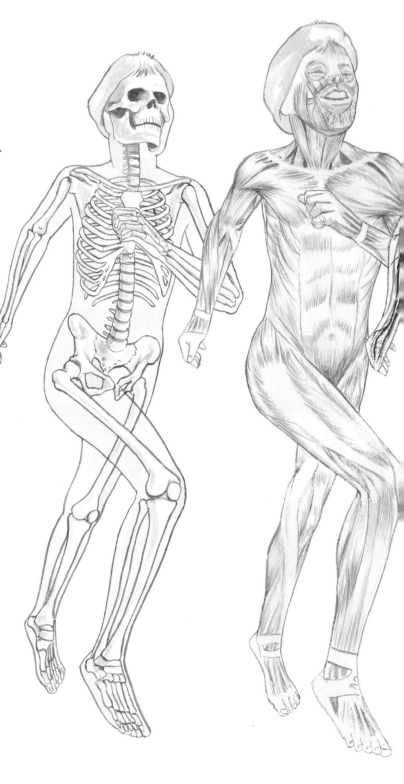

Spare Parts

It is often difficult to find human donors for body parts, so doctors and scientists have invented ways of making a variety of replacements. The first artificial body parts were probably wooden arms and legs. Today, artificial limbs are made from lightweight plastic and metal and look quite lifelike. Electronic hands have also been developed. They are controlled by the nerves and muscles that remain in the arm when an injured hand has to be removed.

Artificial joints can be fitted to mend all sorts of damaged bone joints. Artificial lenses can be placed in the eye, and artificial eardrums can be made for the ear. The tiny bones of the inner ear can be replaced, too.

Diseased or damaged parts of the blood system, such as the aorta and the heart valves, can also be replaced with artificial devices made from plastic and metal. An uneven heartbeat can be corrected by a tiny electronic machine called a pacemaker, which is fitted under the skin of the sick person's chest.

A Better Life

All these operations and devices are designed to help people lead healthier, happier lives. Doctors and scientists are still working hard to come up with even better ways of repairing or replacing diseased or damaged parts of the body.

Body Facts

Our bodies are far more amazing and complicated than any machine that has ever been made! They contain billions of cells, thousands of miles of tubing, and hundreds of muscles and bones — as well as all kinds of finely tuned organs like the brain, heart, kidneys, liver, and lungs.

Brain Power

Although we have invented computers that can work out millions of different things in seconds, our brains can still outwork and outsmart them! Our brains control our bodies by sending out billions of tiny electrical signals every second, and these messages can travel at speeds of 250 miles per hour (400 km/h).

Bone Facts

By the time we grow up, most of us have 206 bones — some people have an extra pair of ribs, bringing the total to 208. Our hands have 27 bones each, and our feet, 26.

▼ Our bodies are made up of four main chemical substances — about 65% oxygen, 18% carbon, 10% hydrogen, and 3% nitrogen. There is also 1.5% calcium and 0.9% iron and phosphorus.

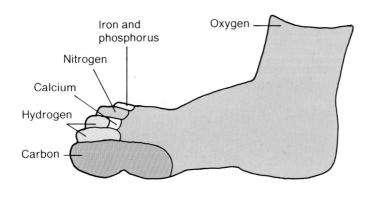

SLEEP AND DREAMING

Sleep is very important to us because it gives our bodies time to grow and repair themselves. The amount of sleep people need varies, though. Young babies grow very quickly, so they need lots of rest — they sleep most of the time, in fact. By the time children are 4, they still need 10 to 14 hours of sleep each night. Adults require the least rest — usually between 6 and 9 hours a night, but some people can live quite happily with only 4 or 5 hours.

During a night's sleep we change position around 40 times and have about five dreams.

▼ People who live in cities walk 7,000 miles (11,000 km) on average during their lives, while people who live in the country cover 28,000 miles (45,000 km)!

All About Eating

Every minute of every day and night our bodies are turning food into energy. An adult man's stomach can hold about $3\frac{1}{2}$ pounds (1.5 kg) of food or drink. A meal takes 10 to 20 hours to pass through his digestive system, and in the course of that time the food travels through nearly 30 feet (9 m) of intestine.

Heating Up and Cooling Down

Your normal temperature averages 98.6°F (37°C), but some people have normal temperatures that are slightly higher or lower. If your temperature falls to 95°F (35°C) you start to shiver, and if it rises toward 100°F (37.7°C) you feel hot and feverish.

Other animals have different body temperatures to us. Birds, for example, have to keep their bodies at around 104°F (40°C).

Sweating helps to cool us down. Normally, we lose nearly 2 pints (1 liter) of body liquid a day through sweating and breathing. People who live in hot countries can lose 3 gallons (11 liters) a day.

Taking Breath

On average we take 20,000 breaths of air into our lungs every day. When our bodies are resting we breathe 10 to 14 times a minute, with each breath lasting 4 to 6 seconds. We usually breathe in about 12 pints (5.5 liters) of air a minute, but we can take in nearly 20 times as much when we exercise.

Pumping Blood

By the time we are adults our hearts beat 70 times a minute to pump blood around our bodies. Other animals' hearts beat at different rates. A mouse's heart beats about 500 times a minute, but an elephant's only beats about 25 times a minute! Our hearts work without stopping or tiring throughout our whole lives.

▼ We swallow a mountain of food and drink during our lives — about 50 tons of food and 13,000 gallons (50,000 liters) of drink!

15,000 miles
(24,000 km)

20,000 miles
(32,000 km)

30,000 miles
(48,000 km)

Useful Words

Antibody A substance made by the body to help it fight off harmful bacteria and viruses, and the poisons these make.

Artery A blood vessel that carries blood away from the heart to the rest of the body.

Backbone Also called the spine. The column of 26 bones (called vertebrae) that runs down the back. It encloses and protects the spinal cord.

Bacteria Microscopic living things, more like plants than animals, but related to both. All bacteria are single cells. Most are harmless, but some, called pathogens, can cause disease.

Blood system The network of tubes through which blood flows around the body. Blood carries nutrients and oxygen to the cells and takes away waste water and carbon dioxide. It is largely made up of a yellowish liquid called plasma. Floating in the plasma are red and white blood cells and tiny bits of cell called platelets.

Blood vessels Tubes that carry the blood the heart pumps around the body.

Brain The body's control center — the organ that keeps the different parts of our bodies working smoothly, and which looks after thoughts, feelings, and memory.

Cartilage The rubbery material that babies' skeletons are made of, most of which hardens into bone during early childhood. The ends of bones that meet at joints are covered with cartilage — it cushions the bones and allows them to move easily against each other.

Cell The smallest unit of life, from which all animals and plants are made. A few animals and plants consist of only one cell, but most are made up of millions. There are billions of cells in the human body. Cells are tiny and most of them can only be seen under a microscope.

CNS Short for central nervous system — the brain and the spinal cord.

Digestion The process whereby the things we eat and drink are broken down until they contain substances small enough to be taken into our blood to feed our cells.

Excretion When the body gives out substances, such as saliva, sweat, and urine.

Fertilization Also called conception. The moment when a sperm cell from a man or male animal enters an egg cell from a woman or female animal. These two cells join to make a new cell which starts dividing and eventually grows into a baby.

Gland A special group of cells which produce substances that the body needs. There are two types. Exocrine glands produce substances excreted by the body, such as saliva and sweat. Endocrine glands produce hormones.

Heart One of the body's most important organs. The heart is a powerful muscle which pumps blood around our bodies without stopping or tiring throughout our whole lives.

Hormones The body's chemical messengers. Hormones are produced by glands and they control many body functions, from our rate of growth to our reactions to fear or anger.

Intestine The long tube that makes up most of the digestive system. There are two parts — the small intestine leads out of the stomach and is where most digestion takes place. The large intestine ends at the anus, the place where the solid waste called feces leaves your body when you go to the toilet.

Joint The place where two bones meet. Some joints are fixed — the bones are fused, or joined together — but others allow the bones to move.

Kidneys The body's main organs of excretion. The kidneys clean the blood by filtering out waste materials and removing any water the body doesn't need. The liquid waste made by the kidneys is called urine. You have two kidneys, one on each side of your backbone in the small of your back.

Liver One of the body's most important organs. The liver receives and processes the nutrients taken into the blood from digested food. It also stores substances needed by the body, and it produces a digestive liquid called bile.

Lungs The spongy organs we use to breathe. You have two lungs, one in each side of your chest. They are made up of tightly packed tissue, nerves, and blood vessels.

Lymph system A set of vessels which carry a liquid called lymph around the body. Lymph contains special white blood cells which make disease-fighting antibodies.

Muscle A special group of cells that can contract, or tighten, and relax, or loosen, to move different parts of the body. The muscles we can control by thinking about them, such as those in our arms and legs, are called voluntary muscles. Others, such as the heart, work on their own and are called involuntary muscles.

Nerve A special group of cells that carries messages between the brain and every part of the body. The messages travel along the nerves in the form of tiny electrical currents.

Nutrients Microscopically tiny substances produced when food is broken down in the digestive system. Nutrients are needed to feed the cells, so they can make the energy we all need to live and grow.

Organ A body part made up of different types of tissue which work together to do one particular job. The heart, the lungs, and the kidneys are all different organs.

Oxygen One of the gases in air. We take oxygen into our bodies when we breathe air into our lungs. Our cells need oxygen to make the energy that keeps us alive. Without oxygen our bodies would die.

Red blood cells Small cells that carry oxygen to the body cells. The oxygen is actually "carried" by a substance in the cells called hemoglobin, which also colors the cells red.

Reproduction The process whereby all living things create new members of their own kind. Nearly all types of cell reproduce by dividing into two new cells.

Senses We have five main senses — hearing, sight, smell, taste, and touch.

Skeleton The framework of bones which supports the body and carries its weight.

Spinal cord The thick bundle of nerves which begins at the base of the brain and runs down the back inside the backbone. Nerves to all the different parts of the body branch out from the spinal cord.

Tissue A group of similar cells which do the same job. Muscles, bones, and nerves are all different types of tissue.

Vein A blood vessel that carries blood toward the heart.

Viruses Microscopically small organisms which cause many different diseases if they get inside our bodies. Viruses grow inside living cells, destroying them in the process.

White blood cells The blood cells that help to fight disease. They are made in bone marrow.

Index